LABELS

The War of Don Emmanuel's Nether Parts
Señor Vivo and the Coca Lord
The Troublesome Offspring of Cardinal Guzman
Captain Corelli's Mandolin
Red Dog
Sunday Morning at the Centre of the World

Louis de Bernières

PUBLISHED BY ONE HORSE PRESS

Text © 1993, 1997 by Louis de Bernières
Illustrations © 1997 by Christopher Wormell
Photograph of the author by Lavinia Trevor

Designed by Kelvyn Smith & Yoke Rasch
Printed by DWJones
First published 1993
Second edition October 1997
This edition © 2001 by Louis de Bernières
ISBN No. 0952 9250 52

ONE HORSE PRESS
The Front Room. 10 The Limes. Cowbridge. Wales. CF71 7BJ.

TO CAROLINE

I was brought up in the days when there was electric light but no television, and consequently people had to learn how to amuse themselves. It was the great heyday of hobbies. People made entire villages out of matchboxes, and battleships out of matches. They made balsa aeroplanes, embroidered cassocks with coats of arms and scenes of the martyrdom of saints, and pressed flowers. My grandfather knitted his own socks, made wooden toys, cultivated friendships with spiders in his garden shed, cheated at croquet, and learned how to produce his own shotgun cartridges. My grandmother's hobby was flower-arranging and social climbing, and my mother played spirituals on the piano in between sewing new covers for the furniture and knitting woolly hats for the deserving poor. My uncle rolled his own cigars from tobacco grown and cured himself. My other grandmother spent happy hours in the garden collecting slugs that she could drop down the grating outside the kitchen, and below a horde of portly toads would eat them before hiding themselves once more beneath the accumulation of dead leaves.

My two sisters had a hobby called 'dressing up'. It consisted of emptying the trunks in the attic, and draping themselves in the extraordinary clothes inherited from previous generations. Then they would go out into

the street, posing as indigent old ladies, and beg coins
from passers-by. One of my sisters, I forget which one,
actually managed to wheedle a florin from our own mother, who failed to recognize her. We spent the florin on
jamboree bags, sherbert fountains, and those dangerous
fireworks called 'jumping jacks'. We set them off all at
once in a field of cows, and sat on the gate gleefully
watching the ensuing stampede. It was only me who got
spanked for it, however, since little girls in those days
were not judged to be capable of such obviously boyish
mischief.

As for me, I evolved through a series of pastimes,
which began as a toddler. My first hobby was saying
good morning. I had a little white floppy hat that I would
raise at any time of day, in imitation of the good manners
of my father, and I would solemnly intone 'good morning'
in a lugubrious tone of voice that I had probably first
admired in a vicar. After that I developed an interest in
drains, and would squat before them, poking with a stick
at the limp shreds of apple peel and cabbage that had
failed to pass through the grate outside the kitchen. I
noticed that in the autumn the leaves turned grey, and I
discovered the miraculous binding qualities of human
hair when it is intermixed with sludge. From this I pro-
gressed naturally to a brief fascination with dog manure,

and am perplexed to this day as to why it was that occasionally one came across a pile that was pure white. Nowadays one never sees such faecal albinism. My wife recalls that as a child she had assumed that such deposits were made by white poodles.

As infancy blossomed into childhood, so my interests multiplied. I made catapults, tormented the cat, pretended to be a cowboy, made boxes with airholes so that I could watch caterpillars become chrysalides, made a big collection of model biplanes and Dinky cars, amassed conkers, marbles, seagull feathers, and the squashy bags in the centre of golf balls. At one point I became interested in praying, and knelt quite often over the graves of our pet animals.

The morbidity of adolescence was to provide me with new joys, such as taxidermising dead animals and suffering endless hours of torment from being in love with several untouchable girls all at the same time. I read every Biggles book I could find, read Sir Walter Scott novels without realising they were classics, memorised hundreds of filthy limericks and rugby songs that I can still recite faultlessly, and discovered that it was possible to have wet dreams whilst still awake.

Many friends pursued arcane hobbies such as collecting cigarette cards and cheese wrappers, shrinking crisp packets in the oven, train and bus spotting, egg blowing, origami, inspecting each others' endowments behind clumps of bamboo, collecting African stamps, and farming garden snails in a vivarium. One of my friends made a hobby of moles, and carved perfect representations of them in softwood with the aid of a scalpel. Another collected one hundred and fifty pairs of wings from small birds that he had shot with an air-rifle. He then suffered a crisis of conscience and joined the Royal Society for the Protection of Birds, becoming eventually one of the few people in this country to have spotted a Siberian Warbler, which was unfortunately eaten by a sparrowhawk before the horrified eyes of thirteen twitchers concealed in one small hide.

Like everyone else I was reduced to extreme torpor and inactivity by the advent of television, but found that I was becoming increasingly depressed and irritable. After a couple of years I realised that I was suffering from the frustration of having no interests in life, and searched around for something to do.

I was in our corner-shop one day when I was most forcibly struck by the appealing eyes of a cat depicted on

the label of a tin of catfood. It occurred to me that a comprehensive collection of catfood labels might one day be of considerable interest to historians of industry, and that to be a connoisseur of catfood labels would surely be a sufficiently rare phenomenon for me to be able to become an eminent authority in a comparatively short time. Instantly I dismissed the idea from my mind as intrinsically frivolous and absurd, and returned home.

An hour later, I was mocking myself at the same time as I was buying the tin with the appealing picture of the cat. With the tin comfortingly weighing down the pocket of my jacket on one side, I returned home once more, and eagerly lowered it into a pan of hot water so that I could soak off the label. I wrecked it completely by trying to peel it off before the glue had properly melted, and had to go out to buy another tin. This time I waited for the paper to float free of its own accord, and carefully hung it up on a blue line that I had stretched from a hot water pipe in one corner of the kitchen over to a hook that I had screwed into the frame of the window. I went out to the stationers and bought a photograph album and some of those little corner pockets which are sticky on only one side. I walked restlessly about the house all evening, waiting for the label to dry, and then could not sleep all night for getting up every ten minutes to go and

test it with my fingers. In the morning, my eyes itching
with tiredness, I glued the label into my album, and
wrote the date underneath in white ink. Afterwards I
went out and bought a hairdryer and two more cans of
catfood.

I was to discover that different manufacturers have
different methods of securing their labels. The easiest
ones to remove are those which are glued with only one
blob, relying upon the rim of the can and their tight fit
to keep them in place, and the worst ones are those
which are stuck in place by means of large smears at
every ninety degrees. On some of them the glue is so
weak that one can peel it off immediately, without soaking, and others are so tenacious that they have to be
immersed in white spirit. I made a comprehensive chart
in order to determine at a glance the best methods for
removing the labels.

I began to accumulate an embarrassment of dela-
belled tins, which grew unmanageable just as soon as I
realised you can obtain them in vast sizes, as well as the
smaller sizes that one commonly finds in supermarkets.
I rebelled against the wasteful idea of simply throwing
them away, and took to giving them away to friends who
possessed cats. They were very suspicious at first and

were reluctant to give the food to their pets in case it turned out to be adulterated, or was in fact steamed pudding, or whatever. They soon came round to the idea, however, when the offerings were unspurned by their cats, as did the owners of cat kennels, to whom I gave the industrial-sized cans. I did notice that many of these people were beginning to look at me askance, as though I was a little mad, and it is the truth that I stopped receiving invitations to parties because my conversation had become monomaniac. I think the worst thing was when my wife left me, saying that she would not move back until I had removed all the albums from her side of the bedroom. The house became a terrible tip because I had no experience of doing the housework, and eventually I had to pay her to come in once a week in order to dust and tidy.

It occurred to me that the easiest way of obtaining labels would be to write to petfood companies and request samples, past and present, but I received no cooperation at all. My first reply was similar to all the others, and ran like this:

> 'Dear Sir,
> Our manager asks me to thank you for your kind letter, and assures you that it is receiving his closest attention.

With best wishes to you and your pussy, we remain, **15**
yours sincerely ...'

Having received this letter, I would hear nothing more.

It may surprise many people that the variety of cat-food labels is virtually infinite. To begin with, every man-ufacturer changes the label fairly frequently in order to modify the targeting of the customer, and to attempt to gain an edge over other brands. Thus a brunette might be changed to a blonde to make a particular food more glamorous, and a Persian cat might be substituted for a ginger moggy in order to give an impression of high class. Shortly afterwards the woman may be changed to a beautiful Asian in order to appeal to the burgeoning immigrant market, and the cat may be changed to a tabby to give it a no-nonsense, no-woofters-around-here, working class appeal. The labels are often changed by the addition of 'special offer' announcements, or, most annoyingly, by 'free competitions' where the competition is on the back of the label so that one has to buy two cans the same in order to have both the obverse and the reverse in one's album.

In addition, every supermarket has its own brand,

and every manufacturer is constantly adding to the range, so that whereas in the old days there was just Felix, Whiskas, Top Cat, etc. each one has flavours such as rabbit and tuna, quail, salmon, pigeon, truffles, and calf liver, each one with changing labels as detailed above. Everyone knows that the food is made of whales slaughtered by the Japanese for 'scientific research', cereals, French horses, exhausted donkeys, and bits of the anatomy of animals that most people would prefer not to eat, but recently the producers have cottoned on to the fact that cat owners tend to buy the food that their cat likes the most, and consequently have introduced greater quantities of finer meat, so that indeed one finds real pieces of liver and genuine lumps of rabbit.

It was when my collection began to go international that I hit the financial rocks. I had been working for several years as a bailiff, a job to which I was well suited on account of my great size and my ability to adopt an intimidating expression. I managed to remain afloat by cutting expenses wherever possible: my car was ancient, I had bought no new clothes for five years, and I cut my own hair with the kitchen scissors. I once sat down with my albums and worked out that I had spent an equivalent of two years' salary on catfood. But I was not broke.

What brought everything to a crisis was a trip to France in pursuit of a debt defaulter. I stopped off in a Champion supermarket and, whilst looking for a tin of cassoulet, I happened upon rows and rows of catfood with beautiful labels, many of them in black, with distinguished scrolly writing upon them. It was love at first sight, and I bought every single type I could find, not just there, but in each Mamouth and Leclerc supermarket that I passed. I found it most touching that the French have many brands that include petits pois and extra fine haricots verts, revealing that French owners anthropomorphically impute to their cats a certain gastronomical delicacy and discrimination equivalent to their own. By misfortune I broke the back axle on the way home, and my hoard of tins eventually arrived by courtesy of the Automobile Association's relay service.

Naturally it became worse and more disastrous by the month. I made frequent trips to France, and returned burdened with cans of Luxochat, Orphée, Poupouche, and Minette Contente. Thereafter I took sick leave from work and discovered the treasure trove of Spain. Not for me the Alhambra: it was Señorito Gatito, Minino, Micho Miau, and Ronroneo.

I came home bursting with happiness and joie de

vivre, planning to cover Germany, and found that my world had fallen apart. My skiving had been discovered, and I was fired from my job at exactly the same time that I received final demands for the electricity, the gas, the telephone, and a reminder to pay my television licence. I sat amongst my albums and my pile of Spanish cans, and realised that I had allowed myself to drift into disaster. I beat myself about the head, first with my hands, and then with a rolled up newspaper. I raised my arms to the heavens in exasperation, moaned, rocked upon my haunches, and smashed a dinner plate on the kitchen floor. Pulling myself together, I made an irrevocable decision to destroy my entire collection.

Out in the garden I built a sizable bonfire out of garden waste, my old deckchairs, and the novelty lingerie I had presented to my wife at birthdays and Christmasses, but which for some reason she had left behind, and went indoors to collect the albums. I found myself flicking through them. I thought, 'Well, I might just keep that one, it's the only Chinese one I've got,' and 'I'll not throw that one away, it's a Whiskas blue from ten years ago,' or 'that was the last one I got before my wife left. It has sentimental value.' Needless to say, I didn't burn any of them; I just got on with soaking the labels off the Spanish cans.

My unemployment benefit did not even begin to cover my personal expenses as well as the cost of acquiring new tins, and I was reduced to buying stale loaves from the baker, and butchers' bones with which to make broth. I had to slice the bread with a saw, and would attempt to extract the marrow from the bones with a large Victorian corkscrew. I became demented with hunger, and the weight fell off me at a rate equalled only by the precipitate loss of my hair from extreme worry. One day, in desperation, I opened one of my tins, sniffed the meat, and began to reason with myself.

'It's been sterilised,' I said to myself, 'and a vet told me that it's treated to a higher standard than human food. O.K., so it's full of ground testicles, lips, udders, intestines and vulvas, but so are sausages, and you like them. And what about those pork pies that are full of white bits and taste of gunpowder? They don't taste of pork, that's for sure. Besides,' I continued, 'cats are notoriously fussy and dainty eaters, apart from when they eat raw birds complete with feathers, and so if a cat finds this acceptable and even importunes people for it, maybe it's pretty nice.'

I fetched a teaspoon, and dipped the very tip of it into

the meat. I raised it to my nose and sniffed. I thought
that in truth it smelt quite enticing. I forced myself to
place the spoon in my mouth, conquered the urge to
retch, and squashed the little lump against my palate. I
chewed slowly, and then ran to the sink and spat it out,
overwhelmed with disgust. I sat down, consumed with a
kind of sorrowful self-hatred, and began to suffer that
romantic longing for death I had not felt since I was a
teenager. My life passed before my eyes, and I had exactly the same kind of melancholy reflections about the
futility and meaninglessness of existence as I had expe-
rienced after Susan Borrowdale refused to go to the cin-
ema with me, and my sister came instead because she felt
sorry for me.

But these cogitations were interrupted by a very
pleasant aftertaste in my mouth, and by the fact that I
was salivating copiously. I picked up the can at my feet,
and sniffed it again. 'All it needs,' I said to myself, 'is a
touch of garlic, a few herbs, and it would really make a
very respectable terrine.'

I took it into the kitchen and emptied it out into a
dish. I peeled three cloves of garlic and crushed them. I
grated some fresh black pepper and some Herbes de
Provence, and mashed the meat with the extra ingredi-

ents. I squashed it all into a bowl, levelled it off with a
fork, and poured melted butter over it so that it would
look like the real thing when it came out of the fridge.

It was absolutely delicious spread over thin toasted
slices of stale bread; it was positively a spiritual experience. It was the gastronomical equivalent of making love
for the first time to someone that one has pursued for
years.

I suffered the indignity of being visited by the same
firm of bailiffs for which I used to work, but my old
mates were kind to me and took only things that I did
not need very much, such as the grandfather clock and
my ex-wife's Turkish carpet. They left me my fridge, my
cooker, my collection of books on the manufacture of terrines and pâtés, my vast accumulation of garlic crushers,
peppermills, herbs, and French cast-iron cookware. I feel
I should explain that I never could do things by halves, I
always have to possess complete collections.

I became extremely good at my new vocation. The
more expensive catfoods made exquisite coarse pâtés
and meat pies [my shortcrust pastry is quite excellent,
and I never leave big gaps filled up with gelatine, as most
pie-makers do]. The cheaper ones that have a lot of cere-

al generally do not taste very good unless they are con-
siderably modified by the addition of, for example, diced
mushroom and chicken livers fried in olive oil. Turkey
livers are a little too strong and leave a slightly unpleas-
ant aftertaste.

The fish-based catfoods are generally very hard to
use. With the exception of the tuna and salmon, they
always carry the unmistakable aroma of catfood, which
is caused, I think, by the overuse of preservatives and
flavour-enhancers. They are also conducive to lingering
and intractable halitosis, as any owner of an affectionate
cat will be able to confirm.

And so this is how catfood, which got me into so much
trouble, also got me out of it. I began by supplying the
local delicatessen, and was surprised to find that I was
able to make over one hundred percent profit. I redou-
bled my efforts, and learned to decorate my products
with parsley and little slices of orange. I learned the dis-
creet use of paprika, and even asafoetida. This spice
smells of cat ordure, but is capable of replacing garlic in
some recipes, and in that respect is similar to parmesan
cheese, which, as everyone knows, smells of vomit but
improves the taste of minced meat.

I discovered that the addition of seven star Greek brandy is an absolute winner, and this led me on to experiments with calvados, Irish whiskey, kirsch, armagnac, and all sorts of strange liquors from Eastern Europe and Scandinavia.

But what really made the difference was printing the labels in French, which enabled me to begin to supply all the really expensive establishments in London: 'Terrine de Lapin à l'Ail' sounds far more sophisticated than 'Rabbit with Garlic', after all. I had some beautiful labels printed out, in black, with scrolly writing.

I have become very well-off, despite being a one-man operation working out of my own kitchen, and I am very contented. I have outlets in delicatessens and restaurants all over Britain, and one in Paris, and my products have even passed quality inspections by the Ministry of Agriculture and Foods. It might be of interest to people to know that my only complete failure was a duck pâté that was not made of catfood at all.

I go quite often on trips across Europe, looking for superior brands of catfood with nice labels, and my ex-wife often comes with me, having moved back in as soon as I became successful. She has become most skilful at

soaking off labels, and is a deft hand with an hachoir. The liver with chives was entirely her own invention, and she grows most of our herbs herself.

I recently received two letters which greatly amused me. One was from a woman in Bath who told me that my terrines were 'simply divine' and that her Blue-point Persian cat 'absolutely adores them' as well.

The other was from a man who said he was beginning a collection of my 'most aesthetically pleasing' labels, and did I have any copies of past designs that I could send to him? I wrote back as follows:

> 'Dear Sir,
> Our manager thanks you for your letter and asks me to assure you that it is receiving his closest attention.'

Naturally I never wrote back again, nor did I send him any labels. Nonetheless I feel a little sorry for him, and anxious on his behalf; it's easy enough to turn cat-food into something nice, but what do you do with hundreds of jars of pâté? With him in mind, I had a whole new range of labels printed in fresh designs, with details of a competition on the reverse.